D1174025

Spearville
Grade School
Library

The TALKING CROCODILE

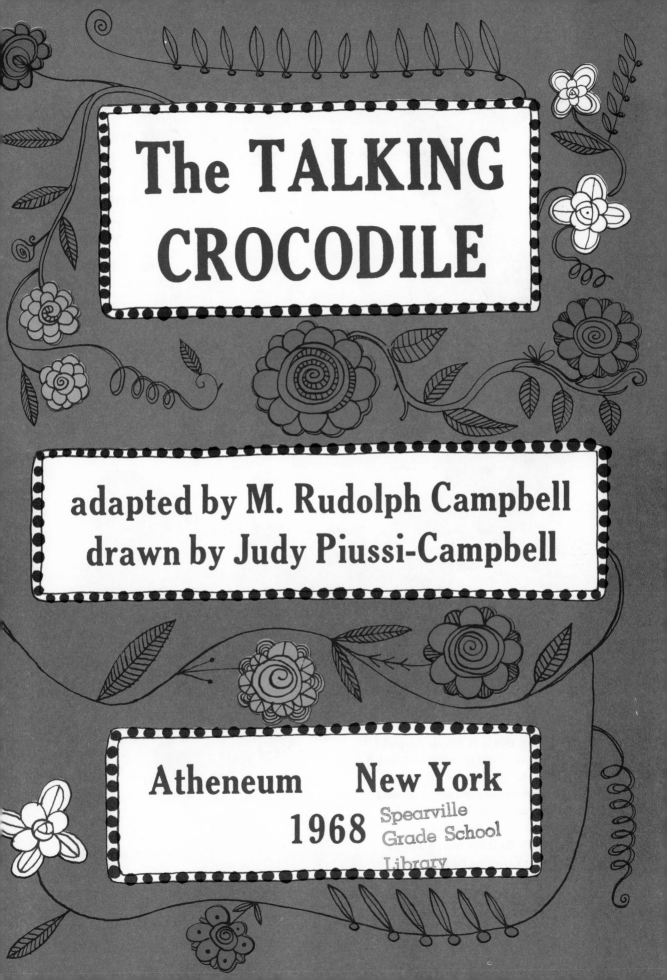

The TALKING CROCODILE

adapted by M. Rudolph Campbell
drawn by Judy Piussi-Campbell

Atheneum   New York
1968

Spearville
Grade School
Library

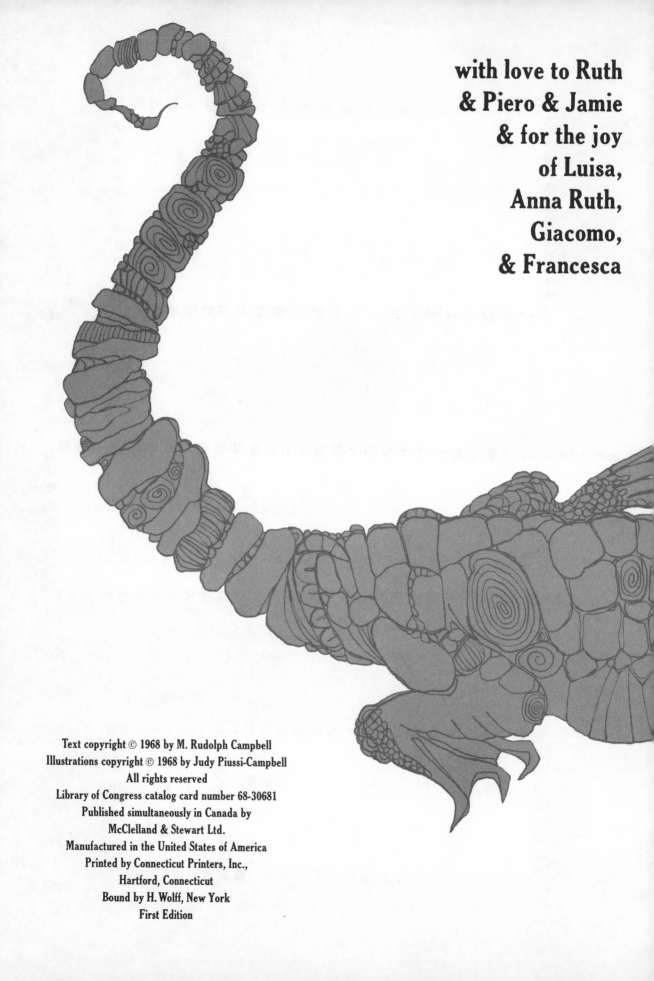

with love to Ruth
& Piero & Jamie
& for the joy
of Luisa,
Anna Ruth,
Giacomo,
& Francesca

Text copyright © 1968 by M. Rudolph Campbell
Illustrations copyright © 1968 by Judy Piussi-Campbell
All rights reserved
Library of Congress catalog card number 68-30681
Published simultaneously in Canada by
McClelland & Stewart Ltd.
Manufactured in the United States of America
Printed by Connecticut Printers, Inc.,
Hartford, Connecticut
Bound by H. Wolff, New York
First Edition

The author,
FYODOR DOSTOEVSKY,
tells this strange tale
& says it is **TRUE**;
else why would he write it?

The time was
January, 1865.
The place, a
Russian city
called St. Petersburg.

My good friends, Ivan & his wife
Elena, lived in St. Petersburg.

One evening, as
was my habit,
I went to
call on them.

Ivan & Elena had read in the newspaper that a crocodile was to be exhibited at the Arcade. None of us had ever seen a crocodile because this was the first one that had ever been

shown in Russia. Crocodiles,
you know, like to live in warm
climates, where there is lots
of water & mud, so that is where
they live, & I don't
blame them, do you?

We all decided to go & see the

**crocodile. Ivan, Elena & I
hitched up their sleigh…**

& soon were at the Arcade.

Ivan was in a happy frame of mind. In fact he even paid for my ticket to the crocodile department.

The place was crowded with folks, all as eager as we to see the strange animal from a far distant land. Once inside we saw the monster in a huge tank, which had about two inches of water.

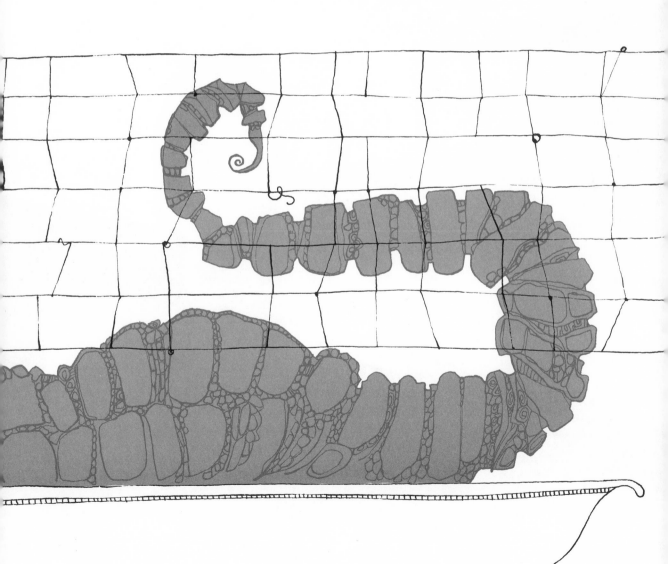

The tank & beast were protected by a flimsy iron grating.

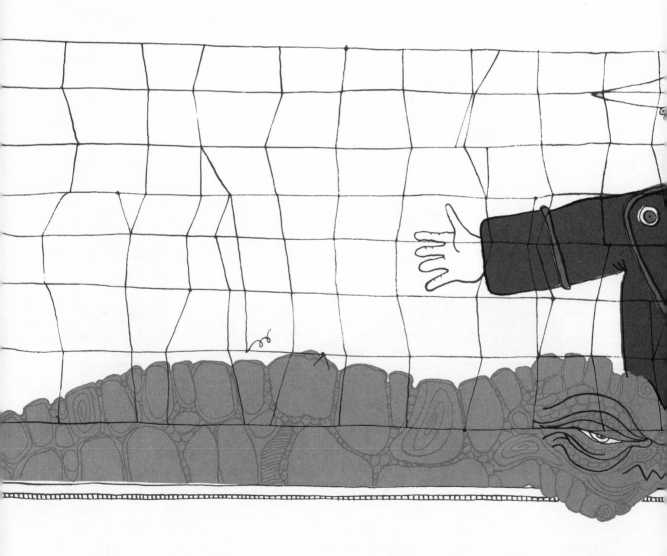

The owner of the
Arcade was a
German named Fritz.
He showed us the
crocodile with much
pride, which was
natural. Wasn't his
pet the first & only
one ever to be seen
in Russia?

Elena was disappointed at first
because the crocodile lay there
like a log.
"Is it alive?" she asked.
"Ach, ja," Fritz said & poked
the loggy thing; calling it
Karlchen—small Karl—a loving
sort of name.

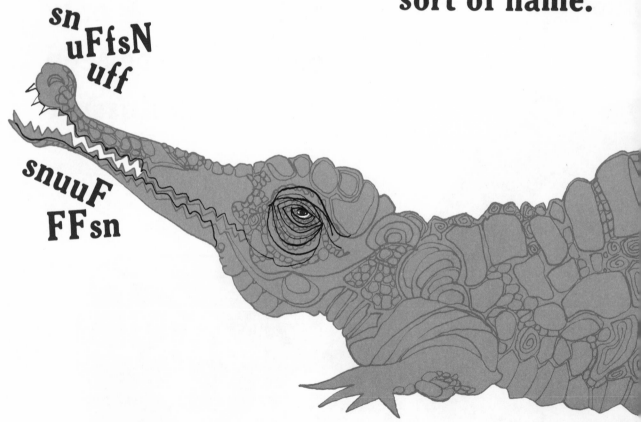

sn
uFfsN
uff

snuuF
FFsn

Karl, when he was poked, snuffed

his snout & switched his tail.

Spearville
Grade School
Library

Elena was frightened, so she & I went to another room where there were parrots

They were
crocodile
name each

& monkeys.
more fun than the
because Elena could
one...

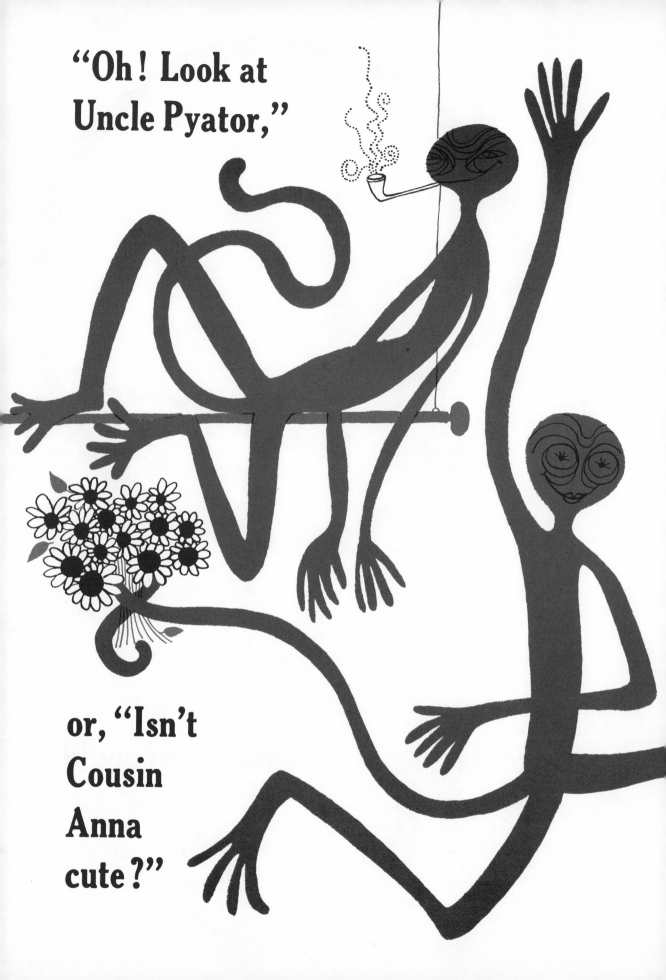

& "That stupid looking one must be Ivan."

We both were enjoying our-selves greatly when suddenly

we heard a piercing shriek from the

Hastening there we

direction of the crocodile tank.

saw a horrible sight.

Ivan, in trying to feed or pet Karl,
& Karl had clutched Ivan around the
proceeded to swallow our poor friend
the air then turning him
around & gulping him down;
feet first,

another gulp

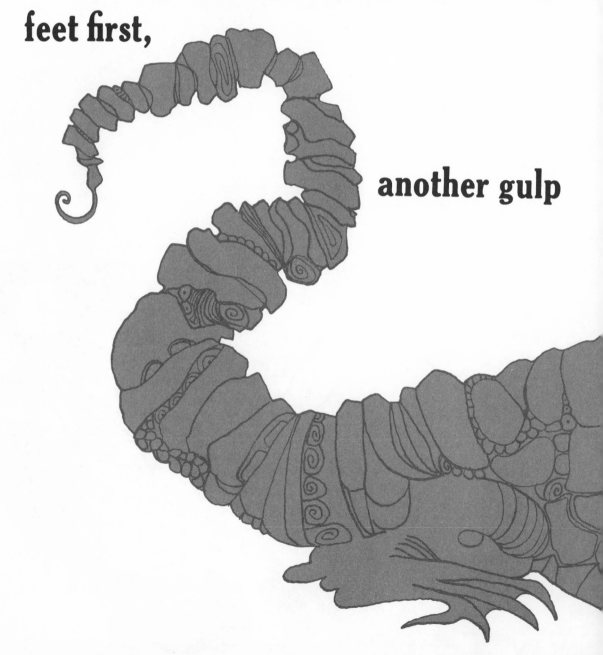

had slipped & fallen into the tank
waist in his awful jaws. He then
whole, first holding him high in

to the waist,
            another

& Ivan was completely inside the monster. There was no trace of him left. Imagine Elena's terror! You would be in the same state if you had the misfortune to witness such a sight. Supposing it happened to you, yourself?

It surely would be most
unpleasant, wouldn't it ? Yes,
it might even be fatal.

Elena begged Fritz to call a
surgeon to excavate in Karl so
that Ivan could be set free.

Fritz answered, "You mean cut a hole in my dear Karlchen? My friend, I am sorry, but an operation cannot be thought of. It would injure his health."

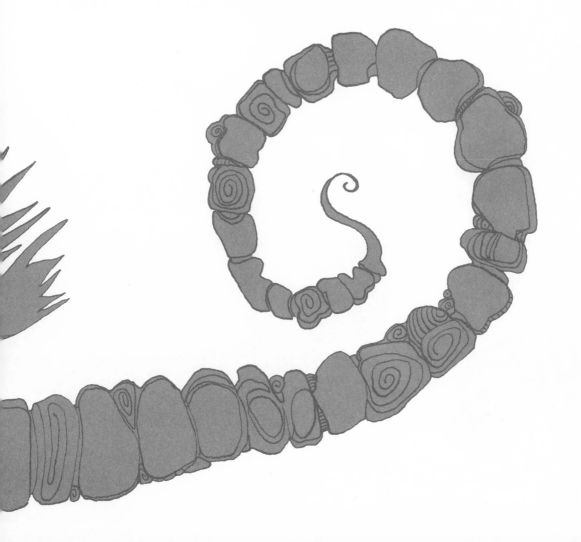

Elena replied, "Ivan was just
How can he now? It wouldn't
would be very expensive to ship
railroad fares & hotel bills!

ready to go on his vacation.
be practical & besides, it
them both. Think of the
How can you be so heartless?"

But Fritz would not change his mind. As we were arguing & pleading with Fritz to do something at once, a voice

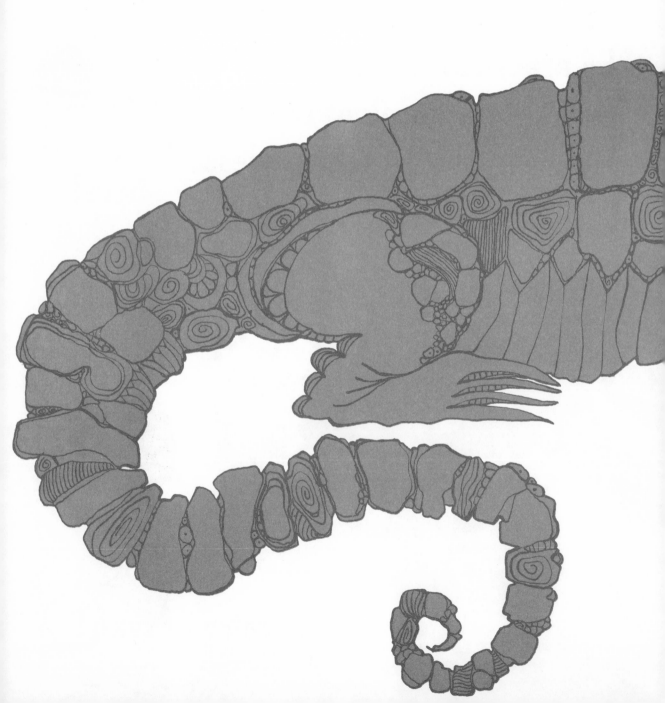

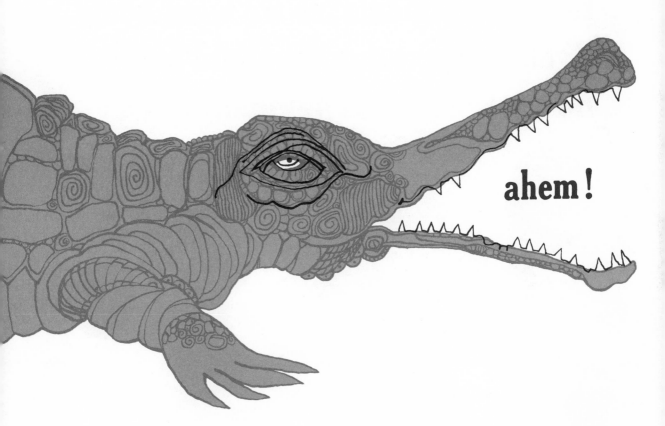

ahem!

**came from the crocodile's mouth!
The voice was muffled, as though
it came through a pillow, but
still it was the voice of Ivan!**

He advised us to see the super-
intendent or other important man.
But it was too late that evening
for appointments, so we went home.
Even the next day we could find
no one who could help poor Ivan.

So of course we visited him at the Arcade every day—being careful to stand just outside the door of the crocodile room so we didn't have to pay the entrance fee.

Ivan seemed to be happy &
to be enjoying his stay in
his odd prison. As time
went on, he became very proud
of himself & thought he
should be getting a reward
from the government for the
scientific facts he could
give about the
inside workings
of crocodiles.

Ivan said

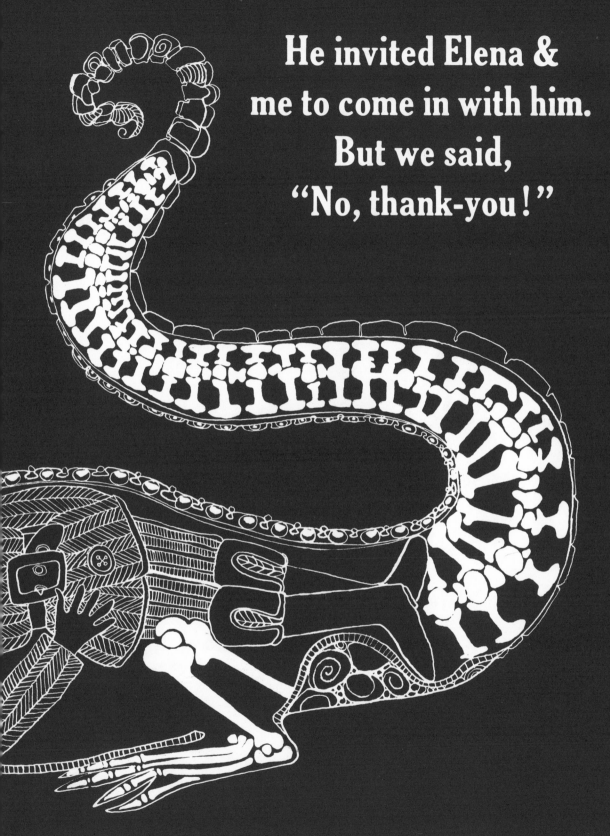

He invited Elena &
me to come in with him.
But we said,
"No, thank-you!"

Karl was hollow & very roomy.

In the end everyone got used to
even began to plan fancy teas with
papers looked forward to writing
Ivan might even make a speech

Ivan's new & unusual home. Elena Karl as Honored Guest. The news- them up. A crocodile at a teaparty! from Karl's mouth!

My
dear
friends...

The teas were a great success, but alas: the lady president of the humane society complained to the chief of police. She said it was bad for Karl's health & especially for his sleep to have such a talkative tenant. The police chief agreed & summoned the tsar's dentist.

After deep thought he pried open

At last they freed Ivan

Karl's jaws & managed to get a rope around Ivan's shoulders.

Then with the help of a dozen strong men,

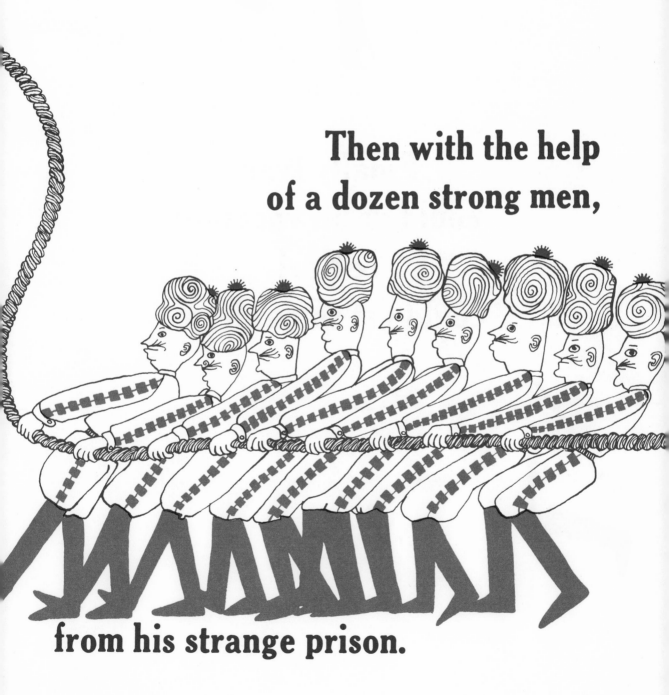

from his strange prison.

**Finally Ivan
could go on vacation
& Karl
could get some sleep.**